Summer in E...

Welcome to the world of Enchantia!

I have always loved to dance. The captivating
music and wonderful stories of ballet are so
inspiring. So come with me and let's follow
Rosa on her magical adventures in
Enchantia, where the stories of dance will
take you on a very special journey.

Special thanks to
Linda Chapman and
Dynamo Limited

First published in Great Britain by HarperCollins *Children's Books* 2009
HarperCollins *Children's Books* is a division of HarperCollins*Publishers* Ltd,
77-85 Fulham Palace Road, Hammersmith, London W6 8JB

The HarperCollins website address is
www.harpercollins.co.uk

1

Text copyright © HarperCollins *Children's Books* 2009
Illustrations by Dynamo Limited
Illustrations copyright © HarperCollins *Children's Books* 2009

MAGIC BALLERINA™ and the 'Magic Ballerina' logo are
trademarks of HarperCollins Publishers Ltd.

ISBN-13 978 0 00 731721 9

Magic Ballerina ™

Summer in Enchantia

Darcey Bussell

HarperCollins *Children's Books*

To Phoebe and Zoe, as they are the inspiration behind Magic Ballerina.

Contents

Prologue

*In the soft, pale light, the girl stood
with her head bent and her hands
held lightly in front of her.
There was a moment's silence and then
the first notes of the music began.
For as long as the girl could remember
music had seemed to tell her of
another world – a magical, exciting
world – that lay far, far away.
She always felt if she could just
close her eyes and lose herself,
then she would get there.
Maybe this time. As the music
swirled inside her, she swept
her arms above her head, rose on to
her toes and began to dance…*

Midsummer Magic

The light was fading, but the summer air
was still warm on Rosa's skin and she
could smell the scent of jasmine blossom in
the air. She was standing with her best
friend, Olivia, in the backstage area of an
open-air theatre. There were stands of seats
on three sides. Rosa could hear the faint
squeaks as people shifted in their chairs.

"Isn't this brilliant?" Rosa whispered to Olivia as they watched the dancers on the brightly lit stage. She tucked her pale blonde hair behind her ears. "I can't wait to go on and dance again."

Olivia nodded excitedly. "Me too!"

Rosa, Olivia and six other girls from Madame Za-Za's ballet school, had been chosen to take part in an outdoor ballet called *Shim Chung*. It told the story of a beautiful girl called Shim Chung who was captured by sailors and held on their boat. They were then shipwrecked, so she went to live underwater with the Sea Dragon King… until she met a handsome prince who, later she married.

Rosa, Olivia and the other girls were dancing the parts of the young mermaids.

They had already been on stage once that
night, doing a dance to entertain Shim Chung,
and now they were waiting for their second
entrance. This dance was Rosa's favourite.
It was a beautiful slow dance to soft,
dreamy music where they had to lull Shim
Chung and the Sea Dragon King to sleep.

It felt so magical to be standing at the side of the stage in the dark, waiting to go on. Being in this ballet had been the most amazing experience of Rosa's life – *well, one of them*, she thought with a smile. For Rosa had a magical secret – the red ballet shoes she was wearing could whisk her away to Enchantia, a land where the characters from all the different ballets lived. The shoes took Rosa to Enchantia whenever there was a problem there that needed solving.

Rosa thought about her best friend in Enchantia – Nutmeg, the fairy of the spices. If only Nutmeg could be there that night to watch her dance in *Shim Chung* for the last time.

The last time. The words echoed in Rosa's head, and she felt a wave of sadness sweep over her as she realised that tomorrow night she would just be at home as normal and the ballet would be over. She and Olivia had done three performances of it and this was their last.

"I wish this ballet could go on for ever," she said, turning to Olivia. "I'm going to miss coming here each night."

"I know. I'll miss it too." Olivia saw Rosa's sadness and squeezed her hand. "But let's not think about that now. If we do, we won't enjoy tonight. We should make the most of it while we're here."

"I guess," Rosa agreed, but the thought ran round and round in her head. No more getting ready in the dressing rooms, no more putting on her green and blue mermaid dress, no more watching the adult dancers chatting and warming up at the practice *barre* at the side of the stage, no more dancing on stage. She sighed, wishing she could take her mind off it. "I think I'll go and get a drink," she said to Olivia.

Rosa went to one of the tables set up for the dancers with cups and jugs of water. She poured herself a drink and walked away from the table. The best way she knew to stop herself from being sad was to dance. She found a quiet place in the shadow of the stands and then, humming the music for the lullaby dance in her

head, Rosa practised a few of the steps – arms up, spin round, three steps forward, pause with knees bent and hands down...

She stopped. She didn't seem able to dance the way she did usually. The sadness inside her was making her feel too heavy.

Rosa bit her lip. She knew she had to pull herself together. The last thing she wanted was to go on stage and dance badly.

Try again, she told herself. *Don't think*

about this being the last time. Arms up, spin round…

Suddenly Rosa felt a familiar tingling in her feet. Looking down, she gasped. Her ballet shoes were glittering as if they were covered with rubies. "Oh, wow!" she whispered. "I'm going to Enchantia again!"

Colours started to swirl about her and the next second she felt herself being lifted into the air and whisked away...

Rosa spun round and round and then the magic gently set her down. As the cloud of colours faded, her feet met something soft and grainy. *Sand!* Hearing the cry of seagulls in the air, she looked about. She was standing on a sunny beach with trees behind her and a blue sea

lapping at the shore. There was a sharp
tang of salt and seaweed in the air and far
out on the water was a large old-fashioned
ship with three masts and rectangular sails.
It was a very different place from the open-
air theatre!

For a moment Rosa remembered the
lullaby dance she'd been about to perform.
Luckily no time ever passed in the human
world while she was in Enchantia, so she
would be back in time to go on stage. She
pushed the thoughts of the ballet to the
back of her mind. Right now she needed to
concentrate on Enchantia.

*I wonder why the shoes have brought me
here?* she thought excitedly. Usually any
problems in Enchantia were caused by the
Wicked Fairy or evil King Rat. Rosa wasn't
keen to meet either of them again, but she
knew she would do whatever she could to
help her friends.

She looked back out to sea, where the
sound of music and shouting drifted across

the waves from the ship. The sailors on board seemed to be having a party. A black flag with a white picture on it was flying from the mast. Rosa looked closer and caught her breath. It was the skull and crossbones. That must mean it was a pirate ship!

Rosa wasn't too sure if she wanted to meet pirates. She was starting to back away uncertainly towards the trees when she heard a voice.

"Rosa! Over here!"

Rosa recognised it instantly. "Nutmeg!" she exclaimed, looking round. She couldn't see her friend. "Where are you?"

Nutmeg poked her head out from round one of the trees. "I'm here!"

Rosa hurried to meet her. As usual,

Nutmeg was wearing a sparkling pink and pale brown tutu and a glittering tiara. Her brown hair was up in a bun and she wore pink pointe shoes.

"It's lovely to see you, Rosa!" she exclaimed.

The two friends hugged.

"So what's going on?" Rosa asked. "Why have the shoes brought me here?"

"Well, we've got a big problem." Nutmeg pointed to the ship. "And it's all to do with those pirates."

Rosa felt a shiver of excitement and fear run through her. "Why? What have they done?"

"Come and sit down," said Nutmeg. "And I'll tell you all about it..."

The Pirate Ship

Rosa and Nutmeg sat down on the soft
sand and the fairy started to explain. "King
Tristan and Queen Isabella decided to have
a big summer garden party for everyone in
Enchantia. They wanted to make it the best
garden party ever and so they arranged for
lots of amazing things to be brought from
all over the kingdom – delicious food and

sparkling jewels and the finest silks for decorating the palace gardens."

"So what's the problem?" asked Rosa curiously.

Nutmeg sighed. "The garden party is set for tomorrow and none of the things that were supposed to be shipped here by sea have arrived. Those pirates over there have been stealing everything."

Rosa glanced across the water. The noise on the ship had got louder and cannons were now being fired.

"We don't know who's their captain or where they are keeping the stolen goods," Nutmeg went on. "I came here to try and find out."

"How are you going to do that?" asked Rosa.

Nutmeg sighed again. "I haven't actually worked that out yet," she admitted.

Rosa considered the problem. "Couldn't you use your magic to get on the ship?" she suggested. Nutmeg could use her fairy magic to get almost anywhere in Enchantia.

"I could," said Nutmeg slowly. "Although it would be very dangerous."

"But you'd definitely find out what's really going on if you did that," said Rosa. "I'll come with you if you like," she offered.

"Are you sure?" Nutmeg said.

Rosa nodded hard. "Of course."

Nutmeg smiled in relief. "Thank you! But before we go I think we should disguise ourselves. If we arrive on the ship looking like this," and she waved at her tutu and

Rosa's green and blue ballet dress, "we'll be captured straight away! I'll make us look like cabin boys. It's a really big ship with lots of pirates, so hopefully no one will notice a few extra crew members." The fairy thought for a moment. "Now what dance should I do to change our clothes?"

Nutmeg could also use her magic to conjure things from a ballet if she did one of the dances from it.

"I need a ballet with sailors in—" Nutmeg went on thoughtfully.

"I know one!" interrupted Rosa eagerly. "Back in my world I'm dancing in a ballet all about the sea. It's called *Shim Chung*. There are sailors in that."

"Oh, of course," said Nutmeg, looking

pleased. "I know Shim Chung. She's lovely, and so beautiful. I went to her palace for a ball once."

Rosa smiled. It was still strange for her to think that the characters in all the different ballets really existed here in Enchantia.

"I know. I'll do a bit of the dance where Shim Chung entertains the captain of the ship." Nutmeg pulled her wand out of her tutu and waved it in the air. Lively music tinkled out. Nutmeg ran forward, paused on her toes, her arms above her head, and then swept her right arm down, turning to the left. She danced swiftly to the right with short steps and moved into an *arabesque*, one leg lifted behind her, before moving on again, repeating the steps.

Rosa watched, entranced. Even though she was wearing a fairy's tutu, Nutmeg seemed to become Shim Chung. Rosa could just imagine her as the young girl. Nutmeg danced out of the *arabesque*, spun around

Rosa and stopped, pointing her wand first at Rosa and then at herself.

There was a silver flash. Rosa gasped and looked down. Her mermaid costume had disappeared and she was now wearing completely different clothes!

She had on a ragged white shirt, a brown waistcoat and dark cropped trousers with a leather belt. Her pale blonde hair was tied up in a bun and hidden by a red scarf.

"Oh, cool!"

Glancing up, she saw that Nutmeg looked

exactly the same except that she had a blue scarf on her head. Her wings were hidden inside her shirt.

"We look just like cabin boys," Nutmeg said, looking pleased. "Well, apart from our ballet shoes. We can't really wear them. Hmmm..." Nutmeg waved her wand again and suddenly they each had a small leather bag attached to their belt.

"We can put our shoes in these," Nutmeg said, patting hers. "Then no one will see them, but we won't have to leave them behind."

Rosa felt relieved. She never liked being parted from her ballet shoes. They always made her feel safe. Untying the ribbons, she slipped her shoes off and put them in her bag.

"Now to get aboard the ship," said Nutmeg.

Rosa ran over and took hold of the fairy's hand as she raised her wand. "Are you ready?" Nutmeg said.

Rosa took a deep breath and nodded. "Pirate ship, here we come!"

Dazzling Diamonds

A cloud of silver sparkles swirled around
Rosa and Nutmeg. The magic lifted them
into the air and whisked them over the
water. Rosa grinned. She loved travelling
by fairy magic! But then, just as they got
closer to the ship, it was as if they had hit
the wall of a bouncy castle. Rosa and
Nutmeg both rebounded backwards.

Suddenly they were no longer spinning;
they were falling down and down…

SPLASH!

Rosa gasped and spluttered as she
plunged feet-first into the sea! Kicking her
way to the surface, she saw Nutmeg's head
popping out of the water at the same time.
"What… what happened?" Rosa cried.

Nutmeg swam over, looking dismayed.
"There must be some spells protecting the

ship. My magic has taken us as far as it can. We can't get on board."

Rosa saw that the ship was just a little way off. Luckily the pirates seemed so busy partying, they hadn't noticed Nutmeg and Rosa landing in the sea nearby. Another cannon boomed into the air and there was a great cheer from the deck. Rosa glanced behind them. The beach looked very far away. "What are we going to do?" she said in alarm.

"Get out of the sea as quickly as possible!" Nutmeg replied. "These waters aren't safe for swimming. There's a hungry sea serpent living in the depths. I'll use my magic to take us back."

Rosa grabbed Nutmeg's hand and the fairy waved her wand in the air. The magic whisked them out of the water and they landed back on the beach by the trees.

"I'm soaked through!" said Rosa, shaking water droplets out of her hair.

"Let's get dry," Nutmeg said, magicking up two large towels. The girls quickly rubbed away the water. Luckily the sun was shining and their clothes soon started to dry out.

"So someone's put spells on the ship,"

said Rosa, looking out to sea. "How are we going to get on board then?"

Nutmeg looked thoughtful. "Maybe I could conjure up a small boat and we could row over?"

"The pirates would be bound to see us coming," Rosa pointed out. She wracked her brains. They couldn't swim or row to the ship, or use magic to get there. If only they could get the ship to come to them! Her thought gave her an idea.

"Could you could magic up a treasure chest, Nutmeg?" asked Rosa. "A really big one the pirates will see from the ship?"

"Yes, I could. But why?"

Rosa grinned. "Because if the pirates see it they're bound to come over in their

rowing boats – the ship would run
aground if they brought it any closer. And
then maybe we can pretend to be in their
crew and get on to the ship that way."

Nutmeg stared at her. "It's very risky."

"I know," said Rosa. "But what else can
we do?" She looked at the fairy's doubtful
face. "Come on. You know we can't give
up!"

Nutmeg nodded. "You're right. OK, I'll
magic up a treasure chest." She waved her
wand and a tune filled the air. It was a
lively hornpipe jig. Nutmeg crossed her
arms in front of her and danced forward
in a straight line, toes turned out, taking
three small skipping steps to the right,
followed by three small skipping steps to

the left. Then she stopped and danced on the spot, putting her heels forward and using her hands as if she were hauling a flag up a mast. It was a very jolly tune. Rosa could feel the music pulling at her feet, urging her to dance.

"Join in!" Nutmeg cried. Rosa didn't need asking twice. She ran to Nutmeg's side and copied the dance. They skipped forward together, arms folded, and then danced on the spot, rocking from side to side as if they were on a stormy sea.

Nutmeg turned a pirouette and pointed her wand. With a flash a wooden treasure chest appeared. It had big metal bands around its sides and it was massive! The top of it reached Rosa's shoulders and it was as long as a car.

"Oh, wow!" breathed Rosa.

Nutmeg heaved open the lid. "Ta-da!"

Rosa gasped. The chest was full of diamonds! She had to shield her eyes as they glittered and sparkled in the sunlight.

"They're not real diamonds," Nutmeg explained. "My magic isn't strong enough to conjure up real jewels. But hopefully the pirates won't realise they're fakes."

"They look real enough to me." Rosa glanced towards the ship and saw the glint of a telescope as it looked towards the beach. "I think they've noticed the chest already! Quick, let's hide!"

The girls ran behind a tree and peeped out. They could see the pirates on the ship all starting to point and look towards the beach where the treasure chest was.

"Let's see what's happening on deck," said Nutmeg. She pointed her wand at the ground. A mist started to form and in the

mist there was a picture. It showed a close-
up view of the pirate ship. Rosa saw the
pirates clustered around the telescope,
pushing each other out of the way, all
shouting.

"Look at it! It's massive!"

"Check out those diamonds!"

"Where did it come from?"

"Who cares!"

Some of the voices sounded familiar.
Rosa peered more closely and caught her
breath. The pirates were a mixture of big
burly men and man-sized mice! Each of
them had a sharp cutlass hanging from
their leather belt. They wore bandanas,
boots and big baggy trousers. The human
pirates were big and muscly and several of

them had wooden legs, but the mice looked even scarier. Their eyes gleamed beadily and when they opened their mouths to shout and snigger they showed off rows of pointed teeth.

"Mice!" whispered Rosa, turning to Nutmeg. "That must mean the pirates are something to do with—"

"What's going on?" snarled a voice on the ship.

"King Rat!" breathed Rosa as a giant rat strode into view. He wore a big black pirate hat and had a long curly wig and a moustache.

"It's treasure, Captain!" one of the pirates said.

King Rat grabbed the telescope. His red

eyes gleamed greedily. "Go on, then! What are you waiting for? I want that treasure now. To the rowing boats, me hearties!"

"Aye aye, Captain!" cried the pirates.

Rosa and Nutmeg watched as the crew quickly lowered three rowing boats from the deck into the water and then climbed down rope ladders hanging over the side of the ship.

"Yo ho ho and a bottle of bilberry wine!" they roared as they started to row towards the beach, their strong arms pulling the boats swiftly through the waves.

Nutmeg waved her wand and the mist vanished. "They're coming!"

Rosa gulped. Now the pirates were actually heading towards them, swearing and shouting, she was beginning to wonder if her plan was such a wise idea. The pirates' curved swords looked razor sharp.

And did she really want to be on a pirate ship with King Rat? But then she thought of the stolen treasure and how sad everyone would be if the garden

party was spoiled. She *had* to do
something! She saw Nutmeg's worried
face, and reached out and squeezed her
hand. "We'll be OK. This plan will work."

The pirates pulled the rowing boats on
to the beach. Jumping out, they ran to the
treasure chest. Rosa took a deep breath.
"Come on!" she hissed to Nutmeg. "Let's
join them!"

Scrub the Decks

The pirates had clustered around the huge treasure chest on the beach. They were so busy looking at all the diamonds that they didn't notice Rosa and Nutmeg creeping out from behind the trees. Rosa wrinkled her nose as she edged into the crowd. It wasn't very pleasant being so close to the pirates. They smelt as if they hadn't washed for a long time. The mouse pirates' fur was greasy and the human pirates had grubby skin. They were all very loud, shouting over the top of each other and elbowing each other out of the way as they plunged their hands and paws into the diamonds.

"We'd better get this chest back to the captain," said one of the mice. Shutting the lid, they started to heave at the chest. Rosa and Nutmeg joined in.

"You, boy!" snapped a voice.

Rosa froze and looked round. A mouse pirate with an eye patch was pointing at her. Had he realised that she wasn't part of the crew?

"M… me?" she stammered.

"Yes, you! I don't recognise you." He

frowned at Nutmeg. "Or you!" His frown deepened.

Rosa had never thought so fast in her life. "That's because… because we were on the ship that this treasure came from," she said. "We were supposed to wait here with it until the people from the palace came to collect it. But… but…"

"We've always wanted to be pirates!" Nutmeg put in quickly. "And when we saw you we hoped that we could maybe join you."

The mouse's eyes narrowed for a moment, but then he seemed to believe them and nodded. "Sensible lads," he grunted approvingly.

"So can we join your crew?" asked Rosa.

"We'll work really hard," Nutmeg
promised.

"You certainly will." The mouse chuckled
nastily. "The last one who didn't ended up
pushed over the side!"

He turned to the other pirates. "We've
got two new recruits to work for us!" he

announced over the noise.

"Oo-ar!" the other pirates growled,
nodding.

"Right, put some welly into it, then!" the
mouse pirate with the eye patch snapped.

Rosa and Nutmeg quickly started
hauling and pulling at the chest with the
others until they got it on to one of the
boats. Rosa and Nutmeg jumped aboard
too.

"Don't just sit there, you little squirts!"
snarled a big burly pirate, thrusting an oar
into each of their hands. "Get rowing, the
pair of you!"

Rosa had never rowed before. She
gripped her hands around the oar and tried
to copy the other pirates, pulling it back

through the water. Soon her arms were aching! Slowly the rowing boat made its way back to the ship, where King Rat was waiting.

"Aha, my lovely treasure!" he said, rubbing his paws together with glee. "Let me see it!"

The chest was hauled up and then Rosa and Nutmeg followed the pirates up the rope ladder and on to the ship. The boats were left behind, bobbing in the water.

King Rat stalked around the treasure chest. "Diamonds!" he said in glee. "Thousands of them!"

"Lucky we spotted them, Captain," said the pirate with the eye patch. "A ship had got past us and left them on the beach."

"And now we have them, One-Eye," said King Rat triumphantly. "More to add to our hoard! We're rich – rich!" He cackled and the rest of the pirates roared in delight.

Rosa glanced around the ship. There were three masts, each with big sails. The centre mast had the skull and crossbones flag flying from the top of it. At the back of the ship, there was a door which had a wooden sign on it saying *Captain's Quarters* and a trapdoor to the brig. In the centre of the ship there were two more trapdoors. Both were open and had steps leading down below the deck. *I wonder if the stolen goods are under there, down one of those flights of stairs*, Rosa thought.

"Oi, you! Boy! What are you doing standing around like a lazy banana!" The pirate One-Eye, snarled. "Get to work! You too, sonny Jim!" he said, grabbing hold of Nutmeg and shaking her.

"What… what should we do?" Nutmeg stammered.

"Go and clean the captain's cabin," said One-Eye. "The cleaning equipment's below the deck." He motioned towards the right-hand staircase.

Nutmeg and Rosa cautiously went down the staircase. There was a large space under the deck where the pirates slept and ate. It was dark down there and smelled of unwashed feet. Rubbish littered the floor. In one corner was a pile of mops, scrubbing brushes, buckets and dusters.

Rosa and Nutmeg took some dusters and headed back on to the deck. King Rat was still admiring his diamonds.

"I guess we'd better go and start cleaning then," said Rosa…

King Rat's cabin was very grand. It had a large bed, a desk, a wardrobe and pictures in gold frames around the walls of King Rat with his wig and pirate coat on. His crumpled clothes were flung on the floor. Nutmeg picked them up gingerly and started hanging them in the wardrobe.

Rosa started to dust the desk. There was a large journal lying open on the top. It seemed to be some sort of diary or log. There was an entry for every day. Rosa read the entries on the open page.

Wednesday 5th June
Weather fair, wind North-Easterly. No sails sighted. Possible sightings of sea beast – her tail seen, but disappeared fast. Pirate crew afraid.

Monster can crush ship in her mighty jaws and eat ten sailors in one mouthful. Hope we do not see her again.

<u>Thursday 6th June</u>

Weather fine, wind Northerly. Still no ships in view, but lookout says he saw monstrous serpent again far out West. No one else saw her. We remain at anchor here to steal more treasure.

"Listen to this!" Rosa said. She read out the log entries to Nutmeg.

The fairy shivered. "I don't like the sound of that. It certainly sounds as if the sea serpent is around – I hope we don't meet it."

"Me too," Rosa agreed. "I want to find

the stolen goods and get off this ship as
quickly as possible."

"Well, none of it is in here," said Nutmeg,
looking around the cabin. "We'll have to
explore the rest of the ship when we can
later."

They finished cleaning the cabin and
went back on to the deck.

One-Eye saw them as they came through
the cabin door. "No lazing around, squirts!
Get mending them there sails!"

He pushed them over towards a pile of
sails.

Rosa and Nutmeg found some big
needles, thread and old bits of sailcloth.
They started patching the sails, but it was
hard work. The sailcloth was very tough

and it was hard to pull the needles through. Rosa's fingers ached, but every time she and Nutmeg paused, one of the pirates would shout at them.

"Finished!" Rosa said in relief as she patched the last hole and cut off the thread.

One of the pirates, a big mouse with a torn ear and a long scar on his forehead, overheard. "If you've finished the sails, get scrubbing the decks."

"Can't we have a rest and maybe something to eat, please?" Nutmeg protested.

The mouse stared at her and then laughed unpleasantly. "Did you hear that, One-Eye?" he called. "These boys want a rest."

"Throw 'em into the sea, Scarface," yelled One-Eye.

Scarface's eyes gleamed. "My pleasure!" He took a step towards the girls.

"No! No!" Nutmeg gasped. "We'll scrub the decks!"

Scarface laughed, a low grating sound. "See that you do!" He swaggered off.

Rosa and Nutmeg found some brushes, mops and buckets under the deck in the living area where the crew slept. After filling the two buckets from a pump on deck, they then found a quiet corner where they began to scrub at the decks. It was hard work and the summer sun was beating down. "I'm really hot," puffed Nutmeg.

"Me too," said Rosa, wiping her arm across her forehead.

"No one else seems to be doing much work," said Nutmeg.

Rosa nodded. As far as she could tell, the pirates seemed to spend most of their time shouting and arguing with each other and occasionally hauling at the sails or moving barrels of bilberry wine and ship's biscuits up from the hold.

To pass the time, Rosa started to tell Nutmeg about the ballet she was performing in, *Shim Chung*. "It's outdoors and there are loads of people watching it each night. I'm a mermaid and I have to do two dances, one where we're entertaining Shim Chung, and one where we dance a lullaby to send her to sleep."

"Which is your favourite dance?" asked Nutmeg.

"The lullaby one," answered Rosa. "Do you know it? It goes like this."

She started to show it to Nutmeg, humming the music as she danced. It began

with the dancers swaying on the spot,
moving their arms from side to side in a
floating movement, and then beginning
to move in a circle, arms at chest height
sweeping round them as they turned
graceful slow pirouettes. Finally the dancers
all stopped, their arms up, spun round and
took three steps forward. They ended the
dance with their knees bent and hands
down, fingertips touching, in front of them.

"That's lovely!" said Nutmeg, joining in.
Getting carried away, Rosa took hold of a
mop and spun round gracefully with it in
a circle, while Nutmeg did a pirouette
with a duster, moving it around as if it
were a piece of delicate seaweed floating
in the water.

She started to hum too.

"Oi!" came a roar. "Stop that right now, you two!" Scarface had heard the humming and was glaring at them. "King Rat won't stand for dancing on this ship. He hates it, he does."

"Sorry," muttered the girls hastily, getting on with cleaning the decks again.

They had just finished when there was a cry of, "Supper time!"

All the pirates cheered loudly.

Rosa felt her spirits lift. She was starving after all the work they had been doing. "Should we put the buckets and mops away first?" she said to Nutmeg.

"No, let's just leave them here," said Nutmeg. "No one will notice. I'm really hungry!"

They went over to the steps that led down to the living quarters. The treasure chest was still in the centre of the ship by the main mast. Every time King Rat came out of his cabin he opened the lid and ran his paws through the diamonds, chortling to himself.

Rosa and Nutmeg followed the other pirates down the steps. They were all queuing around a table where the food was being served.

"Oh," said Rosa when it was her turn. She was given a hard ship's biscuit and a bowl of watery fish stew that looked completely revolting. Rosa was sure she could see a fish's head floating in her bowl.

"Yuck!" she said, pulling a face.

One-Eye looked round.

"I… I mean, yum!" said Rosa, hastily pretending to eat a mouthful. The pirate grunted and looked away. Rosa put her bowl down.

Nutmeg shoved her bowl away too. "Come on, let's go back on deck. It's horrid down here."

They took their biscuits and found a quiet spot on the deck where the ropes were kept near the stern – the back of the ship.

Nutmeg looked at her biscuit. It was the size of a dinner plate. "These biscuits don't look very tasty," she said doubtfully.

Rosa tried a cautious nibble, but her teeth couldn't break off any of the biscuit. It was like biting into a rock!

She looked further up the deck. The mice were managing all right with their sharp teeth, and the human pirates were hacking off bits with their daggers and then chewing hard with their mouths open. But there was no way Rosa or Nutmeg could eat the biscuits at all.

Rosa's tummy rumbled as the delicious smell of sausages and chips wafted up from King Rat's cabin. It was obvious that he wasn't eating ship's biscuits for *his* supper!

"I know," said Nutmeg suddenly. "I've had an idea." She checked no one was looking and then quickly tapped her wand on the floor. There was a small silver flash and two large currant buns appeared, smelling sweetly of nutmeg and cinnamon.

"Thanks!" Rosa said in relief as she and Nutmeg ate their secret supper in silence.

"The sooner we get off this ship the better," Nutmeg sighed, as one of the pirates rolled a barrel of bilberry wine to the front of the ship and all the other pirates clustered round, filling up their tankards.

"We'll wait until everyone is asleep tonight and then have a proper look round for the stolen goods," said Rosa.

However, they didn't have to wait that long. The more bilberry wine the pirates drank, the louder they got, and some of them began to sing while others argued or slumped down on the ground.

"They're all getting drunk," hissed Nutmeg as she and Rosa watched from their hiding place.

"What shall we do with the drunken pirate," sang the pirates, clinking tankards together.

"They're so busy enjoying themselves I bet they won't notice us having a look round," said Rosa. "This is our chance, Nutmeg!" Her eyes shone. "Let's start looking for the stolen goods!"

In the Hold

The two girls got up quietly and made their way to the centre of the ship. The big treasure chest they'd brought on was still there, its lid shut. "Well, we know the stolen goods aren't in the living quarters or King Rat's cabin," said Rosa. "Maybe they're down this other set of steps in the hold."

"Let's go and see," whispered Nutmeg.

They started to tiptoe down the staircase.
A floorboard creaked and they froze,
expecting someone to come and shout at
them. But to their relief, no one seemed to
have heard. They carried on.

At the bottom of the staircase was a
heavy wooden door. Rosa unlatched it and
pushed it open. "Look!" she breathed.

There were chests of jewels, fine silks,
shining satins and delicious food piled high.

"We've found it!" hissed Nutmeg.

They walked into the hold, looking
round in amazement. It was dark under the
deck, but gradually their eyes adjusted to
the dim light and they saw how far back
the room went and how full it was with
stolen goods.

"How are we ever going to get all these things back to shore?" said Rosa.

"If we could get the treasure back on to the beach then I could use my magic to transport it to the palace," said Nutmeg. "But I don't know how we can get it off the ship."

"What *are* we going to do?" said Rosa.

There was a harsh laugh from behind them. "That's just what I would like to know!"

They swung round. King Rat was standing there, flanked by One-Eye and Scarface. "I thought I heard someone sneaking down here," he snarled, his red eyes furious. He turned to One-Eye and Scarface. "Grab 'em and shove 'em in the brig!"

The two pirates charged forward.

"Quick, Nutmeg!" Rosa shrieked.

They ducked around the pirates. The burly mice couldn't move anywhere near as fast. Heart pounding, Rosa darted away from their outstretched paws and nimbly dodged round King Rat. He tried to grab her, but missed and yelled in frustration.

Rosa charged up the stairs with Nutmeg on her heels.

A pirate with a gold earring was about to roll another barrel of bilberry wine from the main mast up to the front of the ship.

"Stop those boys!" hollered King Rat from inside the hold.

The pirate saw what was happening and began a running jump over the diamond-filled treasure chest but just in time, Rosa darted forward, grabbed the lid and flung it upwards like a shield. The mouse hit the lid and bounced off.

"OW!" he shouted.

"Quick, Rosa!" Nutmeg gasped. "Let's try and get in one of the rowing boats!"

But even as she spoke, One-Eye and

Scarface came charging up the steps from the hold. "Not so fast, you little squirts!" Scarface growled.

"The buckets!" Rosa said, spotting the pails of dirty water that they had been using earlier when they were scrubbing the decks. She grabbed one and Nutmeg grabbed the other and, pirouetting round, they flung the dirty water at the two mice as they appeared at the top of the steps. One-Eye and Scarface both spluttered and fell over in surprise.

Two other pirates had heard the commotion and were running towards them now. Nutmeg threw her empty bucket at one of them. It banged into his knees and he turned a somersault and fell on his back with a yell. Rosa chucked her bucket at the other and it fell over his head. He staggered around shouting, "I've gone blind! I can't see!"

"Get to the rowing boats!" Rosa gasped to Nutmeg.

King Rat appeared at the top of the steps. "Stop right there!" he roared and, pulling out his cutlass, he charged towards them.

Rosa grabbed the nearest thing to hand – a small barrel of bilberry wine. She shoved it on to its side and gave it a massive push to roll it quickly towards King Rat. The ship obligingly moved in the water as if the sea were getting rougher. As the ship rose upwards on a wave, the deck tilted and the barrel increased in speed.

"Whaaa!" King Rat shouted as the barrel thwacked into him, knocking the evil rat backwards, straight into the open treasure chest! He popped his head up. He was covered with sparkling stones.

Despite her fear, Rosa giggled. He looked very funny!

The pirates, who had all come running by now, caught sight of him and started sniggering too.

"Stop it! Stop it! STOP IT!" yelled King Rat furiously, his eyelashes twinkling with diamonds. "Get those boys, or it'll be nothing but ship's biscuits for dinner for the whole year!"

At that threat, the pirates roared and charged towards Rosa and Nutmeg, hands out. They were coming from all directions. "There's only one thing for it. Up the rigging!" Rosa shouted. She leapt to the main mast and start to climb the rigging as quickly as she could. Nutmeg followed her. It wasn't easy, because the ship was now moving up and down in the rough sea.

"Where are we going to go?" Nutmeg cried.

"I don't know! Just keep climbing!" gasped Rosa, clinging on to the ropes with all her strength as the pirates started climbing up behind them. Her mind whirled. Sooner or later they would reach the top of the rigging, and then what would they do? There was no escape! But she still kept climbing, faster and faster, higher and higher. She and Nutmeg were both light and nimble and they could move much faster than the heavy, cumbersome pirates.

"Now where?" said Nutmeg as they reached the top of the main sail. There was nowhere else to go, so they edged

out along one of the
wooden spars at the
top of the sail, until
they were above the
rolling waves.

"I... I don't
know," said Rosa,
panic rising inside
her. She glanced
down. The pirates
and King Rat were
gathered on the
deck, yelling up at
them, while two
more pirates slowly
climbed the rigging
towards them, eyes

gleaming, daggers between their teeth.

"We're completely trapped, Rosa!" said Nutmeg. "Whoa!" she cried, hanging on as the ship tossed upwards on a large wave. "And it doesn't feel very safe up here!"

"Why's it so rough suddenly?" Rosa exclaimed. There was no wind blowing the sails. The waves shouldn't be as big as they were. Still, she didn't have time to worry about that now. The ship plunged down a wave and she felt her fingers slip on the ropes. She tried to cling on, but she didn't have a proper grip. The ship bucked like a horse and suddenly Rosa lost her footing and was flung off the rigging.

She heard Nutmeg yell and saw her in the air too. They both cried out as they started to fall…

Escape!

Rosa fell through the air, her hands reaching out for anything to grab hold of, but closing on nothing. *I'm going to land in the sea!* she thought fearfully. But just then she bumped backwards into something soft and strong. It was the sail! She heard Nutmeg gasp as she hit it too. Rosa started to slide down it at top speed on her back.

All she could see
was the blue sky
and the sea. The
rush of the air in
her ears
drowned out
every other
sound – it was
like being on a
giant slide! Rosa felt Nutmeg
grasp her hand and pull her
up into a sitting position.

"Whee!" shouted the fairy
as they slid and bounced
down the sail, their head
scarves coming off and their hair
blowing free.

The fear at being captured or falling disappeared in the sheer rush of speed. "Wowwwww!" Rosa yelled, clutching Nutmeg's hands as they bounced on to the lowest sail.

"We're going to land in the rowing boats!" cried Nutmeg. "Look, Rosa!"

Rosa realised Nutmeg was right. Directly beneath them was one of the small rowing boats, bobbing next to the ship like a cygnet behind the mother swan! On the deck of the ship she could see the pirates yelling and King Rat waving his cutlass.

"Here we go!" cried Rosa, as the end of the lowest sail approached fast.

They flew off the end of the sail, fell through the air and then landed on the piles of rope in the bottom of the rowing boat. It was a bit of a bump, but Rosa was so relieved not to have ended up back on the ship that she didn't care. She struggled up, but was almost thrown overboard as the little boat pitched violently on the waves. "Quick, Nutmeg! Let's get rowing!" she said, crouching down again.

Rosa seized the oars while Nutmeg threw off the rope that was holding the rowing boat to the pirate ship. It had taken the pirates a few moments to realise what was happening, but now they all rushed to the side of the ship and leaned over.

"They're not boys after all! It's that dratted girl and the blasted fairy!" roared King Rat over the hullabaloo. "Stop them from getting away!"

Hearts pounding and breath short in their throats, Rosa and Nutmeg started rowing as hard as they could. But the waves were big and the girls weren't strong enough to pull through the stormy sea. Rosa glanced round to see the pirates swarming down the rope ladders and jumping into the two other rowing boats.

The pirates were big and strong and were rowing through the waves pretty quickly. The two boats chased Rosa and Nutmeg until they closed in on either side of their boat.

"What are we going to do?" said Rosa, as the pirates got closer and closer.

"I'll magic us away," said Nutmeg. "Grab my hands, Rosa!"

Rosa dropped the oars, but just before she could take the fairy's hands, Scarface took a flying leap into their boat! He pinned her arms to her side, pulling her away from Nutmeg.

"Let me go!" Rosa shouted, trying to kick him.

"Not likely!" Scarface laughed. "King Rat will reward me for this!"

"Go, Nutmeg!" Rosa yelled. "Save yourself!"

"No, I won't leave you," protested Nutmeg. She began to lunge at Scarface, but it was too late. One-Eye had jumped in from the other boat and grabbed her too.

Rosa and Nutmeg struggled, but there was nothing they could do. *We're caught,* thought Rosa in dismay. *Totally and utterly caught!*

The pirates rowed the girls over the tossing waves back to the ship. They pushed them up the rope ladder and on to the deck. King Rat was waiting for them, his eyes burning fiercely. Rosa felt a flicker of fear, but she wasn't going to show that to King Rat. She faced him bravely.

"So, you thought you could sneak on to on my ship, did you?" King Rat snarled. "You were after my treasure, weren't you?"

"It's not your treasure!" Nutmeg shouted, stumbling as the ship rolled in the water. "All of those goods belong to the King and Queen of Enchantia."

King Rat laughed. "Not any more, they

don't. It's mine." He clenched his front paws triumphantly. "All mine!"

"What are you going to do with the prisoners, Captain?" demanded Scarface.

A slow smile spread across King Rat's face. He twirled his long whiskers. "I'm going to make them walk the plank!"

The pirates erupted into a mighty cheer. "Hooray!"

"No!" Rosa gasped, looking out at the stormy sea.

"The plank!" shouted King Rat gleefully to his crew.

Two pirates dragged out a wooden plank and set it on the deck so that it jutted out over the ocean. A groaning sound seemed to come from under the waves.

"What's that?" said Rosa.

The pirates looked mystified.

"Come on! Come on!" chivvied King Rat.

"But, Captain," began Scarface. "What's that noise?"

"No buts! Get on with it! It's just the noise of the wind."

"But there isn't any wind…" One-Eye began, but thought better of it as King Rat shot him a fierce look. The pirate helped shove the girls up on to the plank.

The ship heaved in the rough sea. Rosa struggled to keep her balance on the plank. "You can't do this!" she shouted to the evil captain.

King Rat strutted up and down the deck, curling his moustache round his paw. "Just watch me."

"We'll drown!" protested Nutmeg.

"So? You should have thought of that before you snuck on to my ship. I'll be glad to see the back of the pair of you. Now walk the plank!" Neither Rosa nor Nutmeg moved. King Rat drew out his cutlass and jabbed the sharp point towards them. "Go on!"

"Yeah, walk the plank!" the pirates chorused.

Rosa and Nutmeg edged a little way along the plank. The pirates cheered. "Can't you use your magic to whisk us away?" gasped Rosa.

"No. The plank is attached to the ship and my magic won't work here because of

King Rat's spells," groaned Nutmeg. "Once we're in the sea I might be able to, but it's so rough we might not be able to hold on to each other. I won't go without you." She looked close to tears.

The ship swayed. The girls grabbed each other's hands.

What are we going to do? Rosa thought, but for once, she was completely out of ideas.

"Hold on to me as tightly as you can," said Nutmeg as they reached the end of the plank. "Try not to let go!" Rosa took a deep breath and got ready to jump.

"One…" said Nutmeg, "two…"

But before she could say *three*, there was a loud roar and a bright pink sea serpent burst out of the waves right in front of them!

The Lullaby Dance

The giant creature reared up out of the water. She had a long slender neck and head and her big dark eyes were screwed up. She opened her jaws, showing off big pointed teeth as she made a loud groaning noise.

"It's the monster from the deep!" yelled the pirates.

They scrambled away from the edge of the boat as quickly as they could. Nutmeg and Rosa ran back to the deck, jumping quickly off the plank.

The serpent thrashed her head from side to side and waved her tentacles about, groaning.

"Oh, my goodness! So that's what's been making the waves!" exclaimed Nutmeg, hanging on to the railings at the side of the deck. "It must be why the sea has been so rough even though there's been no wind. The sea serpent must have been moving about beneath the surface. Oh, poor thing, she looks like she's in pain!"

Rosa was torn between feeling terrified and curious. "In pain?" she echoed.

Nutmeg nodded. "Look at her."

The sea serpent made another loud pitiful roaring noise and her eyes blinked open for a moment. Rosa realised Nutmeg was right. The serpent's eyes were full of pain, but despite that they looked large and kindly. She didn't look vicious at all.

"Argh!" yelled the pirates in terror. "It's going to eat us!"

King Rat hastily pushed two pirates in front of him. "If you're hungry, eat them, not me!" he shouted to the serpent.

"Don't be silly. Can't you see she's friendly? She's not going to eat anyone!" cried Nutmeg, but King Rat and the pirates were too busy panicking to listen.

The serpent's vast tail came up and

splashed down on the sea, making the ship
swoop up and down again on the waves.

"What's the matter with her?" Rosa asked.

"I don't know," replied Nutmeg. "If we
could think of a way to calm her down then

we could find out."

An idea jumped into Rosa's mind. "Would dancing work? We could do the dance I was showing you – the one that lulls the Sea Dragon King and Shim Chung to sleep."

Nutmeg's face lit up. "It's worth a try."

Rosa started to hum. Nutmeg waved her wand and the music that matched the tune Rosa was humming filled the air. It was dreamy and slow.

King Rat poked his head up from behind the pirates. "Urgh! No! Not music and dancing!"

Trying to ignore him and the swaying of the boat, Rosa and Nutmeg started to dance. They swayed on the spot, moving their arms from side to side, and then they began to move in a circle, turning slow, dreamy pirouettes.

Rosa glanced at the monster. She had stopped thrashing about and her eyes were opening. She blinked down through her

long eyelashes and stared at the girls as
they continued to dance, turning every
three steps, their arms floating around
them.

"I think it's working!" gasped Nutmeg as
the monster began to wave her head and
neck in time with the music.

Rosa lost herself in the dancing. It was
easier now the serpent had stopped moving

as much and the ship was steadier. She glanced at the serpent again and saw that the creature was sinking back into the water, her vast head coming lower and lower until it was level with the ship. It was the strangest feeling ever to be dancing on a pirate ship, while a giant sea serpent stared at her!

The monster opened her mouth, but didn't roar. This time, she yawned dreamily, a slight whimper of pain escaping from her.

The music came to an end and, as the girls stopped with their hands in front of them, the serpent looked at them sleepily and then breathed out a long sigh. "Ahhhhhhhhh."

Nutmeg walked slowly forward. "H... hello."

The sea serpent blinked. "Hello," she rumbled. "I liked your dancing, little fairy."

"Thank you," said Nutmeg. "I'm Nutmeg and this is my friend, Rosa."

Rosa waved cautiously.

"My name is Esmeralda," announced the sea serpent.

"What's the matter with you, Esmeralda?" Rosa asked, going forward to stand beside Nutmeg. "You sound like you're hurt."

Esmeralda nodded. "One of my teeth is sore. Your dancing made me feel better..." She broke off and gave a loud groan. "But it's starting to hurt again now." She lifted her head back and roared, "It hurts. It really hurts!"

Rosa stared. What could you do to help a sea serpent with toothache?

Esmeralda started to thrash her tail around again and the ship began to toss up and down on the waves.

"Stop! Please stop!" cried Nutmeg in alarm. But Esmeralda was shaking her head so hard she didn't hear her.

"Let's dance again, Nutmeg!" cried Rosa, but the ship was moving too violently for them to begin. Every time they tried to stand up, the ship swung up and down and they fell over.

"Watch out!" yelled Nutmeg as a particularly large wave hit and the ship stood almost on its end.

Rosa and Nutmeg both grabbed on to the side railings just in time to stop themselves from tipping into the ocean. "Esmeralda! You've got to stop it!" cried Rosa. "Please! You'll sink the ship!"

But the sea serpent didn't hear. Her tail hit down against the ship's railings on the other side of the deck, shattering them in one blow.

"Abandon ship, me hearties!" she heard King Rat shout as the ship righted itself. "Rats, mice and men first!"

"Shouldn't that be women and children first?" cried Nutmeg, grabbing Rosa's hand as the pirates started swarming over the sides of the ship and leaping for the boats.

They were blubbing and yelling.

"Not on my ship!" snarled King Rat, pushing her back. "Stay out of the way, you annoying fairy! Don't you even think of getting into one of our boats."

"But the ship's going to sink if this goes on!" cried Nutmeg. "You can't leave us here."

King Rat chortled. "Watch me!"

And he ran to the side of the ship and jumped overboard!

As he did so, the ship gave another great heave. Rosa and Nutmeg grabbed one of the masts. A barrel of ship's biscuits fell on its side and rolled down the deck, its lid smashing off. As the big biscuits rolled out all over the place, Rosa had an idea.

Letting go of the mast, she ran over to the

barrel. They had to get Esmeralda to calm down again so they could talk to her. They couldn't dance with the ship tossing and heaving like this on the waves, but maybe there was another way.

"What are you doing, Rosa?" cried Nutmeg.

"This!" Rosa grabbed the remaining biscuits from the barrel and started throwing them like Frisbees into the sea serpent's open jaws. Esmeralda spluttered in surprise as she crunched down on them.

"Ow!" she roared, opening her mouth again. As she did so a big white tooth rolled out, attached to a biscuit!

For a moment Esmeralda opened and shut her jaws, and then a look of astonishment crossed her face. Her thrashing slowed down. "The pain!" she rumbled in surprise. "It's stopped!"

"Your tooth has come out," Rosa told her. "That's why the toothache has gone."

"Oh, well done, Rosa!" said Nutmeg, hugging her. "How do you feel, Esmeralda?"

The sea serpent worked her jaws up and down and from side to side. "Much better, actually," she commented.

Rosa breathed out a sigh of relief.

"What a brilliant idea," Nutmeg said.

"I just meant to calm Esmeralda down," admitted Rosa. "I didn't mean to make her tooth fall out. Those biscuits really *are* hard!"

Esmeralda smiled. "Thank you for helping me." She peered down. "Now what are we going to do about *them?*"

The ship had settled now and the girls suddenly became aware of the sound of yelling from beneath them. Rosa peered over the side. The pirates were splashing about in the water. The waves had turned every rowing boat upside down. Even King Rat was floundering around, his wig soaked through and flopping to one side.

"I could always eat them," said Esmeralda thoughtfully, "although I don't think they look as if they would taste very nice – I really prefer eating seaweed."

It was a tempting offer, but Rosa quickly shook her head. "No, you'd better not. Maybe you could you put them in the brig for us, though?" she asked, looking at the trapdoor on the deck that led down to the ship's prison.

"Certainly!" said Esmeralda, swooping down and scooping three pirates out of the water in one go. "It's the least I can do!" She swung them over the deck. Rosa and Nutmeg pulled the trapdoor open and

Esmeralda dropped the yelling pirates inside, before swinging back for some more.

Soon all of the pirates were in the brig. Last of all, Esmeralda scooped up a very wet and bedraggled King Rat.

"Let me go!" he yelled, shaking his fist. "You can't do this to me!" he shrieked at Rosa.

She grinned. "Just watch us! Thanks, Esmeralda!"

The sea serpent dropped King Rat into the brig on top of the rest of the pirates.

"But I'm cold and wet and hungry!" wailed King Rat from inside the brig.

"There's plenty of ship's biscuits to eat!" said Rosa, tipping a load of them down inside.

Nutmeg slammed the trapdoor shut and bolted it. "That should keep them safe." She grinned. "Me hearties!"

Rosa giggled. "Now we just need to get the ship back to the shore," she said. "Then we can unload the King and Queen's treasure and magic it back to the palace for the party."

"Hooray!" said Nutmeg. Then she frowned. "Though how *are* we going to get it to the shore? I don't know how to sail a ship."

"Maybe I could help you out there, too," Esmeralda volunteered. "I could push you back to the beach."

"That would be brilliant!" said Rosa. "Thank you!"

"My pleasure. You certainly helped me out, little human. If it wasn't for you, my tooth would still be hurting and goodness knows what damage I would have caused. Here we go!"

The sea serpent dived down and hauled up the anchor with her teeth. Dumping it on the deck, she gave the girls an almost

shy look. "Would… would you mind
dancing for me while I push the ship along?
It's just, I love to watch dancing and I
hardly ever get to see any."

"Of course we will!" exclaimed Rosa.
"We love dancing too!"

Nutmeg waved her wand and the music
for the jig they had danced earlier flooded
out. The girls began to dance the hornpipe
on the deck, skipping forward, backs
straight, arms folded. Smiling happily,
Esmeralda pushed the ship gently through
the waves and, with the first stars of the
night shining overhead and the lively music
in their ears, Rosa and Nutmeg danced on.

Pirate Prisoners

When they reached the beach, Esmeralda pushed the ship all the way up on to the sand until it would move no further. Then she unloaded the treasure from the hold, her long tentacles snaking down the steps and plucking the chests out one by one. At last, everything King Rat and his pirates had stolen was piled up on the sand.

"Thank you so much!" Nutmeg said
gratefully to Esmeralda. "Now I can use my
magic to whisk everything back to the
palace and we can have the garden party
tomorrow after all."

"I wish you could come," Rosa said,
patting the sea serpent's neck.

Esmeralda smiled. "I will think of you all
having a lovely time, and be happy. I prefer
it in the sea." She glanced at the brig. "But
what about those perishing pirates?"

Rosa and Nutmeg looked at each other.
"We're going to have to let them out at
some point, I suppose," said Nutmeg
reluctantly.

Rosa walked over to the brig trapdoor
and banged on it.

"Let us out!" groaned King Rat. "I feel seasick!"

"You can only come out if you promise that you won't be a pirate any more," said Rosa.

"I promise!" wailed King Rat. "I'm fed up of the sea and I never want to see a ship's biscuit ever again. I won't be a pirate any more. I'll be good, I'll be ever so good!"

"OK, then we'll let you out," said Rosa, reaching for the trapdoor bolt.

She heard King Rat give a low chuckle, and hesitated.

"Maybe it would be safer if I let the pirates out in the morning when you and Nutmeg have got safely away," Esmeralda said thoughtfully. "Then if any of them

have any funny ideas of trying to stop you,
they'll have me to deal with."

"Noooooooo!" yelled King Rat.

Rosa smiled. "Thanks, Esmeralda. That's
a great idea!" She turned to Nutmeg. "Shall
we go to the palace?"

"First let's change our clothes," said
Nutmeg, looking down at her tattered and
wet cabin boy costume. "We can't go back
looking like this."

They climbed down to the sand then
Nutmeg spun round and round before
stopping and pointing her wand first at
Rosa and then at herself. There was a bright
flash of light and Rosa looked down to see
that her cabin boy clothes had changed
back into her green and blue dress and her

ballet shoes were back on her feet. "That feels better," she said, pointing her toes with a happy smile.

Nutmeg was back in her tutu again, her wings sparkling in the starlight. She twirled round. "Time to get back to the palace and tell everyone else that the party tomorrow is on!"

Rosa ran over to the treasure and took Nutmeg's hands. "Bye, Esmeralda!" she called, waving to the sea serpent. "Thank you for all your help!"

"Goodbye, my friends!" rumbled the sea serpent. "Thank you for stopping my toothache – and for dancing for me!"

"I'll make sure I come and dance for you again soon," promised Nutmeg. She waved her wand. Silver sparkles spun around them and they and the stolen goods were whisked away.

The girls arrived in the Royal Palace courtyard. As the sparkles cleared, several servants came hurrying out. They stared in amazement at all the stolen treasure.

"Where are the King and Queen?" asked Nutmeg. "And my sister, Sugar?"

Before anyone could answer, a beautiful fairy in a sparkling lilac tutu came to the doorway.

"Sugar!" cried Nutmeg, hurrying forward to hug her older sister, the Sugar Plum Fairy.

"Oh, Nutmeg!" Sugar gasped. "You did it! You've brought everything back!"

"With Rosa's help," said Nutmeg, turning round and holding out her hand.

Rosa ran over eagerly. "Hi," she smiled at Sugar.

"Hello, Rosa. So what's been happening?" asked Sugar. "Where did you find all this? How did you get it? Who were the pirates?"

"It's a long story," Nutmeg told her.

"Come inside," urged Sugar. "I know the King and Queen will want to hear it. They'll be so pleased to see you and to find out that their treasure has been found! They've been wondering whether they should cancel the garden party tomorrow. Come on!"

Rosa and Nutmeg followed Sugar into the palace. She led the way to a grand drawing room where King Tristan and Queen Isabella were talking anxiously to each other by a large fireplace.

"You're back!" cried King Tristan, on seeing Nutmeg.

"And Rosa too," said Queen Isabella. Her face lit up. "Have you come to help us, Rosa? We've got a real problem."

Rosa curtseyed. "No you haven't, Your Majesty!" She smiled. "Nutmeg and I have solved it!"

The King and Queen looked astonished. "But how?" asked the King.

Rosa and Nutmeg told the story of everything that had happened.

"Thank you, both of you," Queen Isabella said, taking Nutmeg and Rosa's hands. "You've saved the day again."

Rosa and Nutmeg beamed.

"You must be worn out and very hungry," the Queen went on. "I'll have some food brought here and two bedrooms made up for guests. You will stay for the party tomorrow, won't you, Rosa?"

Rosa looked at her feet. She never had any say over when the shoes decided to take her home. "I'd love to, but I might get whisked away."

"I hope you don't," said Nutmeg.

Rosa hoped so too! She was keen to go and dance in the ballet back at home, but the garden party sounded like it was going to be amazing. She snuggled down in her chair as the Queen organised some sandwiches, fruit and ice cream to be brought in for her and Nutmeg.

I don't know how long I'm going to be here for, she thought, *but I'm going to make the most of every single moment!*

The Garden Party

Rosa woke up the next morning, still in
Enchantia, having spent the night in a
massive four-poster bed. She jumped up
and ran to the window. As she threw back
the heavy gold curtains, the sunlight
streamed in. Her window looked down on
to the gardens. Below them every servant
in the palace seemed to be bustling about,

putting out tables for food and shady
tents made of the beautiful silks that Rosa
and Nutmeg had brought back. Strings of
glittering jewels were being hung from
tree to tree, catching the sunlight and
sparkling. Sugar was there in a lilac dress,
dancing around and waving her wand.
Every time she touched a tree trunk, sugar
plums popped on to its branches. Rosa
breathed a happy sigh. It looked like the
garden party was going to be just as
wonderful as the King and Queen had
planned.

Rosa looked round and saw that a dress
had been put in her room. It came to just
below her knees and was made of dark
pink and white striped silk with a pink

sash. Rosa quickly got dressed and put on her ballet shoes.

Just as she was tying the ribbons, there was a knock at the door and Nutmeg came in. She was also wearing a summer dress; hers was pale pink with a light brown stripe. Her long hair was free from its usual bun. She hugged Rosa. "I'm so glad you're still here. That dress looks gorgeous on you."

"You look lovely too!" Rosa said.

"Come on, let's go and help!" said Nutmeg.

Smiling happily, they ran downstairs.

By lunchtime, the party was in full swing,

the gardens bustling with people. Waiters were handing out glasses of iced fruit punch and dishes of ice cream. The tables were laden down with all sorts of delicious food – sandwiches, iced cakes, cherry buns, candied fruit from all over the land and sculptures made out of golden spun sugar. There was a stall set up handing out candyfloss, circus performers walking on stilts and juggling, and best of all, a band playing wonderful music to dance to.

Rosa had a brilliant time. She and Nutmeg danced and danced, then stopped to have something to eat and then danced some more. Rosa enjoyed every second; in fact she enjoyed it so much that she forgot

all about going home.

But as the sun started to sink down in the sky, she felt her feet tingling. "The shoes!" she gasped, looking down at them sparkling. "Oh, but I don't want to go! I don't want all this to stop."

"Don't worry," said Nutmeg. "I bet you'll be back here for another adventure soon!"

Rosa realised she was right. This adventure might be about to end, but then another was surely not far away. That was how it went. She grinned, feeling suddenly better. "Bye, Nutmeg! See you again soon, I hope!"

"Bye!" called Nutmeg.

A rainbow of colours swirled around

Rosa. She felt herself being lifted into the
air and whisked away…

Rosa was set down gently. The haze of
colours cleared. She was back in the quiet
shadows in the backstage area of the
open-air theatre. She shook her head,
trying to adjust from being in the crowded,
sunny gardens of the Royal Palace. Her
summer dress had changed back to her
mermaid costume. It was almost like it had
all been a dream. Feeling a bit strange, she
walked back to Olivia who was still
standing near the entrance to the stage.

"Hi," Olivia whispered. She looked
concerned. "Oh, Rosa, don't be sad."

Rosa remembered what they had been talking about before she went to Enchantia. Olivia must be thinking she was upset about the ballet ending.

"There'll be other ballets for us to be in," Olivia told her. "And other fun things will happen."

Rosa smiled. "It's OK. I know. One adventure has got to end before another one can start." She thought back to everything she had learned in Enchantia and twirled round. "But right now, this one is still going on and I'm going to enjoy every minute of it!"

When the music started that signalled their

entrance, Rosa and Olivia ran onstage.
The other girls came on from the opposite
entrance and they met in the middle. Shim
Chung and the Sea Dragon King were
sitting on thrones. The music slowed and
Rosa and the others began to perform the
lullaby dance.

Sway to the right and left, right and left, arms out, floating through the water...

The music swelled around her and Rosa stopped thinking about the steps. She just danced, swept away by the music, lost in the moment.

As the dance ended, the girls stopped, perfectly balanced, feet in third position, fingertips touching. Joy swept over Rosa. It had gone brilliantly! The audience clapped loudly. Rosa beamed around at the audience, dazzled by the moment. And then as the music changed, feeling as if she were sparkling with happiness, Rosa danced off the stage with the others, heading for her next adventure.

Magic
Ballerina

We hope you enjoyed
your special Summer
in Enchantia with
Rosa!

*

Join all your
magical
friends
at

www.magicballerina.com

Magic Ballerina™

ISBN 978 0 00 728607 2

ISBN 978 0 00 728608 9

ISBN 978 0 00 728610 2

Join Delphie on her adventures in the magical world of Enchantia

ISBN 978 0 00 728617 1

ISBN 978 0 00 728611 9

ISBN 978 0 00 728612 6

Magic Ballerina™

ISBN 978 0 00 730029 7

ISBN 978 0 00 730030 3

ISBN 978 0 00 730031 0

Join Rosa on her adventures
in the magical world of Enchantia

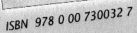

ISBN 978 0 00 730032 7

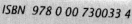

ISBN 978 0 00 730033 4

ISBN 978 0 00 730034 1

Darcey Bussell

Buy more great Magic Ballerina books direct from HarperCollins
at 10% off recommended retail price.
FREE postage and packing in the UK.

Coming Soon...

Holly and the Dancing Cat	ISBN 978 0 00 732319 7
Holly and the Silver Unicorn	ISBN 978 0 00 732320 3
Holly and the Magic Tiara	ISBN 978 0 00 732321 0
Holly and the Rose Garden	ISBN 978 0 00 732322 7
Holly and the Ice Palace	ISBN 978 0 00 732323 4
Holly and the Land of Sweets	ISBN 978 0 00 732324 1

All priced at £4.99

**To purchase by Visa/Mastercard/Switch simply call
08707871724** or fax on **08707871725**